THE LITTLE DUCK

A Random House PICTUREBACK®

THE LITTLE DUCK

Story by Judy Dunn

Photographs by Phoebe Dunn

RANDOM HOUSE NEW YORK

15 16 17 18 19 20

One morning in early spring a little boy was fishing in the pond near his farm. Again and again he threw out his line and pulled it in. At last he caught a fish.

The boy gathered his things to go home. Suddenly he saw something nestled in the tall grass at the pond's edge. It was an egg—a duck's egg. The little boy carried the egg home with him.

He placed the egg in an incubator so it would keep warm. Every day the boy turned the egg over as gently as a mother duck.

Finally, after twenty-eight days of waiting and watching, the boy heard something peeping and pecking inside the egg. The shell cracked . . . and broke open. Henry, the little duck, was hatched.

Henry did not look at
all as the boy thought
he should.

His feathers were wet, and
they stuck to his body.
His feet were enormous.

Finally, after twenty-eight days of waiting and watching, the boy heard something peeping and pecking inside the egg. The shell cracked . . . and broke open. Henry, the little duck, was hatched.

Henry did not look at
all as the boy thought
he should.

His feathers were wet, and
they stuck to his body.
His feet were enormous.

The little duck stood up on his big orange feet. He tried a few small steps.

Then he stretched his spindly wings and wiggled them as fast as he could. He began to get dry and fluffy.

Getting hatched is hard work. Henry was tired. He put his head down beside his empty shell and went to sleep. When Henry woke up his fluffy yellow down was completely dry. Now he looked like a duck.

After a few days the boy
placed him in a wading pool.
It was time for the little
duck's first swim. Henry
tried hard to paddle.
But the more he paddled,
the deeper he sank.

Ducks cannot float without
oil on their feathers. Baby
ducks usually get this oil
from their mother's feathers
when she sits in the nest
with them.

But Henry's mother was
an incubator. He would
have to wait until his own
oil glands began to work
before he tried to swim
again.

The boy quickly scooped Henry up from the bottom of the pool and wrapped him in a towel. Henry was shivering and sputtering.

The boy was afraid he would catch cold.
So he set the hairdryer on "warm" and
dried Henry's feathers in no time.

When the little duck was dry
again, he found a cozy resting
place on the broad back of the
family dog. Together they dozed
in the sunshine.

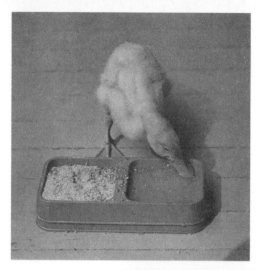

Through the summer Henry kept growing. The boy fed him cracked corn and duck mash. The more Henry ate, the bigger he grew.

One day as Henry was standing beside a puddle, his reflection showed stiff white feathers growing over his yellow down.

Suddenly Henry's voice began to do something new. While he was small, *peep peep* was all he said. But now strange noises came out when he opened his beak:
Peep peep squank.
Peep quonk. Peep quack quack quack.

Henry was growing up.

During the summer Henry followed the boy all around the farm.

Sometimes the boy was busy. Then Henry looked for other friends. One day he waddled down the hill and into the barnyard. He quacked at the hen. But the hen did not care about ducks.

He quacked at the rabbit. The rabbit listened,
but did not say anything. When Henry quacked
at the goat, the goat leaned over and butted him.
Finally Henry went back home.

Summer turned into autumn and the boy had to go to
school. Without anyone to play with, Henry had nothing
to do all day. He tried to swim in his blue plastic pool.
But the pool had become too small for Henry.

On weekends the boy stayed
home. Then Henry was happy.
He had a playmate.

And sometimes, on warm
winter days when the boy
was away, his grandfather
would rock Henry on the
porch.

But still Henry seemed
lonely. He needed a special
friend. The little duck was
almost grown up.

One bright morning in early spring Henry waddled off the porch.

He was a handsome grown-up duck now, with a beautiful curled feather at the tip of his tail.

Henry walked straight down the hill, past the barnyard, and across the meadow.

Suddenly Henry stopped. He opened his beak in a loud quack. Before him was a wide, deep pool of water—much wider and deeper than his blue plastic pool at home. Henry had found the pond.

In the middle of the pond, spreading its wings, was the first duck Henry had ever seen.

As fast as he could Henry paddled out to meet
the new duck. It looked almost exactly like
Henry. But it did not have a special curl at the
tip of its tail.

The duck was a girl. She quacked at Henry.
Henry had found his special friend at last.

Soon Henry and his friend had
an egg of their own, nestled in
the tall grass beside the pond.